A FIREFLY BOOK

Published in the U.S. in 1996 by:
Firefly Books (U.S.) Inc.
P.O. Box 1338
Ellicott Station
Buffalo, New York 14207

Original title: Cachettes et Camouflages
Copyright © 1990 by Les éditions du Raton Laveur.
English text copyright © 1993 by Scholastic Canada
Ltd. Published by arrangement with Scholastic
Canada Ltd.

6 5 4 3 2 1   Printed in Canada   6 7 8 9/9

Cataloguing in Publication Data

Caumartin, Francois
  [Cachettes et camouflages. English]
  Now you see them, now you don't

Translation of Cachettes et camouflages.
ISBN 1-55209-007-8

1. Title. II. Title: Cachettes et camouflages. English

PS8555.A869.C3213 1996   jC843′.54
C96-930446-3   PZ7.C38No 1996

NOW YOU SEE THEM, NOW YOU DON'T

François Caumartin

English text by
David Homel

FIREFLY BOOKS

Simon was a famous hunter, and he had a collection of trophies from all over the world.

But his collection was not complete.

One day he packed his bags and set off for faraway lands.

From the tropics to the equator, the word went out among the inhabitants. They all wondered what they should do.

The Council of Animals held a meeting and decided to find a way to escape the danger.

"This calls for action," the elephant trumpeted.

"There's strength in numbers," the rhinoceros grunted.

"Let's find a solution!" the lion roared.

No sooner said than done. They took out paint and brushes, and everyone pitched in to find the best hiding places and the cleverest camouflage.

They worked so well that when Simon arrived, he was surprised to find only flowers, rocks and empty fields.

He looked as hard as he could, but there wasn't a wild animal in sight.

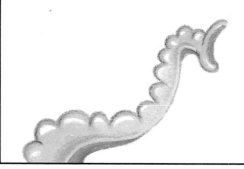

He crossed savannas and plains without finding a single wild beast. Not even a rhinoceros. Though he did come across a few cows that glanced at him as he went by . . .

. . . along with some pink flamingos that watched him nervously.

But they were hardly worth the effort for a big-game hunter like Simon!

For days, weeks, months he travelled, through country after country.

He explored a thousand caves, crossed a thousand valleys, beat the bushes along a thousand rivers . . . but it was no use. The land was empty and abandoned.

"Let's look a little deeper in the forest," Simon decided next.

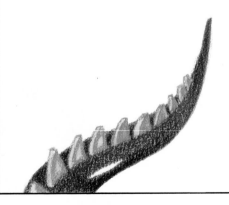

But even in the heart of the jungle Simon found nothing. Discouraged, he leaned against a tree to rest a while.

"I'd better face the facts," he said to himself. "There's no big game to hunt here."

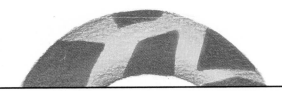

So Simon went home, without having seen a single tiger, elephant, rhinoceros, hippopotamus, crocodile, giraffe or lion.

What a disappointment!

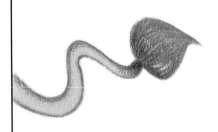

That was a great day for the animals, and they got together for a grand celebration. As a souvenir of Simon's visit, they composed this little refrain:

All you hunters, hear our song,
Don't bother bringing guns along.
Instead of shooting that giraffe,
Why don't you take a photograph?

9700

W

Caumartin,
    Francois.
Now you see
    them, now you
    don't